# ReacH!

Written by Lisa Gammon Olson

Illustrated by Lauren Rutledge

*At Eifrig Publishing, our motto is our mission —*
*"Good for our kids, good for our Earth, and good for our communities."*
*We are passionate about helping kids develop into caring, creative, thoughtful individuals who*
*possess positive self-images, celebrate differences, and practice inclusion. Our books promote*
*social and environmental consciousness and empower children as they grow in their communities.*
*www.eifrigpublishing.com*

© 2022 Lisa Gammon Olson

Printed in the United States of America

Published for Balance America with the support of Eifrig Publishing,
PO Box 66, Lemont, PA 16851, USA

For information regarding permission, write to:
Rights and Permissions Department,
Eifrig Publishing,
PO Box 66, Lemont, PA 16851, USA.
permissions@eifrigpublishing.com, +1-814 954 9445

Library of Congress Cataloging-in-Publication Data

Olson, Lisa Gammon
Reach! / by Lisa Gammon Olson,
illustrated by Lauren Rutledge
p. cm.

Paperback:     ISBN 979-8-218-04806-8
Hard cover:    ISBN 979-8-218-04740-5
Ebook:         ISBN 979-8-218-04741-2

[1. Society--US 21th Century - Juvenile Fiction.]

I. Rutledge, Lauren, ill. II. Title

26 25 24 23 2022
5 4 3 2 1
Printed on recycled acid-free paper. ∞

**Mission Statement**

Balance America is a group of lifelong friends with varied political orientations, taking the commonalities that bind us together as Americans to start the process of healing our country for future generations while holding our elected officials accountable. Together we will reunite our beloved lake community, our Badger state and this great nation. We ARE the Sons and Daughters of Lombardi!

Once upon a time,
on a board high above,
nine babies were swaddled
with clouds and with love.

The babies were happy,
all dimples and charm.
Their world...perfect and balanced
kept them safe from ALL harm.

As they started to grow
they LOOKED at each other!
While not related by blood,
they were sister and brother.

They laughed at their sameness,
eyes, knees, and ten toes!
Chubby cheeks, hands for holding,
each a pert little nose.

In preschool, they learned
to be KIND and to share.
When one child was hurting
they ALL showed their care.

Their first interactions...
blocks, swings, hide and seek!
They started to notice
what made EACH unique.

Moira! Max, Jed and Hector!
Josie! Jemma's MY name!
Alastair, Madi, Daisy!
No two were the same.

"I like to play pirates!"
"I like to make art!"
They still played together...
but sometimes apart.

As the children grew older,
peer pressure crept in.
"You're SO good at baseball."
"You're fat!"  "You're too thin."

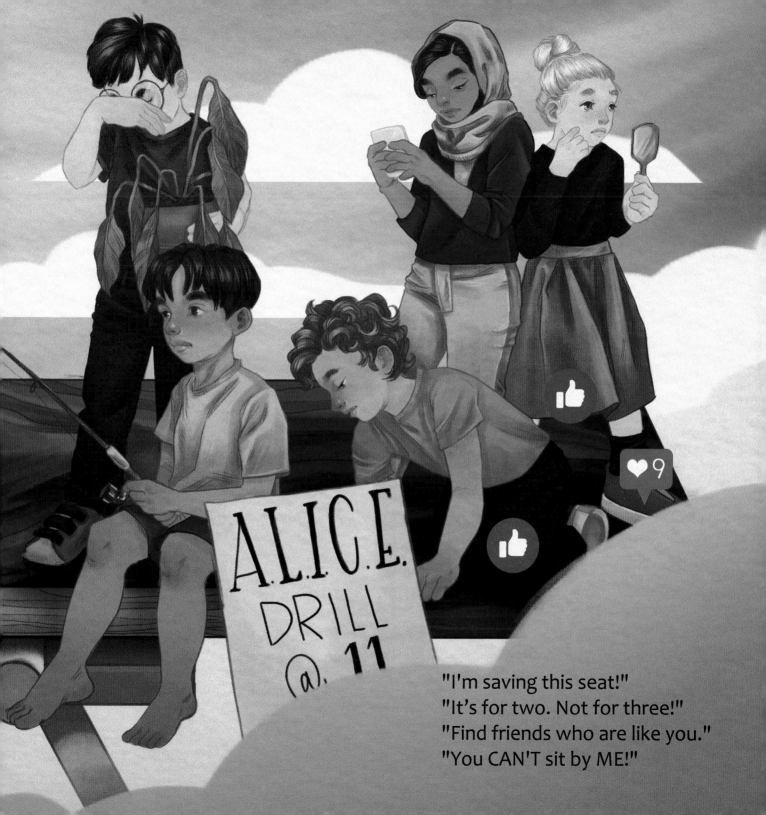

"I'm saving this seat!"
"It's for two. Not for three!"
"Find friends who are like you."
"You CAN'T sit by ME!"

Hearts started to harden...
Kind thoughts tucked away.
Opinions from others
divided their ways.

With their structure unbalanced, the board started to crack as they SHOUTED...picked sides grew apart and attacked.

Emotions were raw...
there were shouts and name-calling.
But they stayed unaware
of the dangers of falling.

These nine righteous humans
out to settle the score,
didn't notice their board
had deep fractures...GALORE!

Their egos took over
and they focused on ME.
They forgot about kindness.
They forgot about WE.

"I need to make money."
"MY ideas are BEST."
"If you don't think just like me,
 you don't pass the test!"

The baby with the dimples...
The one with the curl...
FORGOT their love for each other
in this emotional swirl.

The boy who played pirate...
The girl who LOVED art...
The kids on the seesaw...
were now worlds apart.

Both sides became separate,
far left...and far right.
When the board SNAPPED in half,
they were FROZEN with fright.

"Stop fighting!" "Don't move!"
"HELP!" they heard a voice call.
"My hands...they are slipping!"
"I'm starting to fall!"

"Give me your hand!"
"We need to rescue our friend."
"If we don't work together
THIS might be our end."

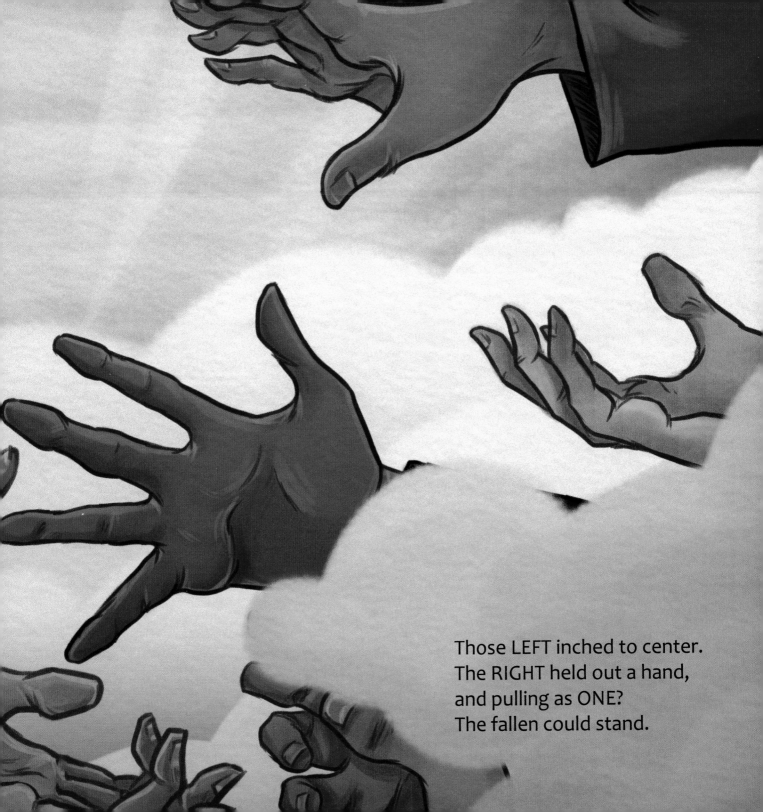

Those LEFT inched to center.
The RIGHT held out a hand,
and pulling as ONE?
The fallen could stand.

We've all been so selfish.
We've forgotten to share.
We've stopped loving each other
and forgotten to care.

We need to move forward,
as one...as a TEAM.
Let's bring balance back
to our home... to our beam.

Remember...Our diversity
is what makes us strong.
As a country we RISE
when ALL feel they belong.

United? We stand.
Divided? We fall.
If we look for equality,
we'll SEE justice for ALL.

Our kids! They ARE watching.
They are emulating our deeds.
Leave them footsteps worth following...
and sow them new seeds.

We've time to change tactics...
to reach across ... to reach high.
By working together?
The limit's the sky!

*Instilling the love of reading,
promoting kindness, empathy
and a respect for our planet
one book at a time.
~ Lisa Gammon Olson*

*Dedicated to all the children in America, from Karen
& Mike McKanna in honor of their grandchildren, Evan & Ivy McKanna, and
Cameron & Shelby Elkins. Thank you, McKanna Family, for making this book possible.*

*Special message to: Luke Porter, Riley Isis Collins, Madi Thomas, Theodicia Powers,
Max Westegaard, Oliver Larsen, Ava Calderon, Maleyia Zimmerman, Walter Hause,
Elaina, Evelynn & Jodi Stieve, Henry & Calvin Ganser and Anderson Curti*

*ALWAYS BE KIND & use your talents to make this world a better place.
Follow in Balance America's footprints and finish what we've started.
www.balance-america.com*

*Midwestern gal who loves
animals. And cheese.
~ Lauren Rutledge*